TEN LITTLE
UNICORNS

Library of Congress Cataloging-in-Publication data is available
ISBN: 978-1-955077-49-1 (Paperback) | 978-1-955077-53-8 (Hardback) | 978-1-955077-54-5 (eReader)

10 9 8 7 6 5 4 3 2 1
First printing edition 20201

East 26th Publishing
Houston, TX

www.east26thpublishing.com

TEN LITTLE
UNICORNS

By Paige Clough
Illustrated by Stephani Pappas

EAST 26TH
PUBLISHING

A herd of TEN LITTLE UNICORNS,
each with a distinct personality.

ONE,
TWO,
THREE...

Let me tell you how this little herd came to be.

Step by step, building a herd takes time and patience.

Shelter, water, food, love, friendship,
and knowing their place in the cadence.

It is important to allow them space to be their own part of the balance.

Each unicorn contributes to the group
with their own gifts and talents.

SUNFLOWER

Blazing fire of fear, he comes out of nowhere
and finds a field sprayed with golden sunflowers.

A refuge from fright, he stays the night,
closing his eyes as he waits for the sun's light.

Walking through the maze of sun rays,
flowers kiss him from head to toe.

Sprinkled by pollen dust and touched by the sun,
he knows it's time to go.

Calmly, he returns to face the day,
leaving the field of flowers to play.

GOOD KNIGHT

Lay down your sleepy head in your comfy, cozy bed.

The Good Knight unicorn waits for you to fall asleep.

For he dances and prances in your dreams.

He battles the scary things and jumps through fiery rings.

He sings a lullaby from way up high and brings your dreams to the sky.

The Good Knight unicorn takes you on a ride–
your guide across the starlit sky.

He keeps you safe all through the night.

Lay down your sleepy head in your comfy, cozy bed.

BUTTERFLY

Up high, down low,
I flutter and fly everywhere I go.

Looking for a peaceful place,
I find it in your amazing grace.

Changing and growing at my own pace,
I enjoy every moment without haste.

On our journey, up ahead a split in the path reveals itself.
One side well-discovered; the other a new page on the shelf.

Which path shall we flutter upon?

Forging our way anew, we create our own balance.
Let's try the new path and see what happens.

FOUR,
FIVE,
SIX...
the herd doubles in size.

Discovering friendship as they graze on the lush green pasture.
Each falling into step amongst the others under ripe skies.
Barns and paddocks built to protect the group by a friendly rancher.

RAINBOW

Volcanoes erupt fire and ash.
Earthquakes shake the ground in the west.
Chaotic twisters swirl across flat lands.

Super storms travel across a lightening-streaked sky,
With hints of rolling thunder nearby.

Rain drops soak the pastures deep.

Wait!
Says the Rainbow unicorn.
There are promises to keep.

Look here!
A kaleidoscope of hope appears across the sky.

These rainy days have gone away.
Do you see the promise of a new way?

Everything is going to be okay
A promise for a better day.
Everything will be okay.

FREEDOM

Firecraker! Firecraker! in the sky.
Here to celebrate the fourth of July.
Let the bells ring. Let freedom sing.
Grateful for grass-strewn blankets and liberty!

WEDDING

Dreaming of her wedding day, the Wedding unicorn plans.

First comes love.
Then, will you marry me?

Say YES!
Then save the date and don't be late.

Here comes the bride all dressed in white.
The groom waits with bated breath ahead.

Wedding guests are dressed to impress.
Fragrant flowers fill the chapel.
Sealed with a kiss, let's have some cake and celebrate!

SEVEN,

EIGHT,

NINE...

the herd is almost complete.

The first unicorn makes sure there is plenty for all to eat.

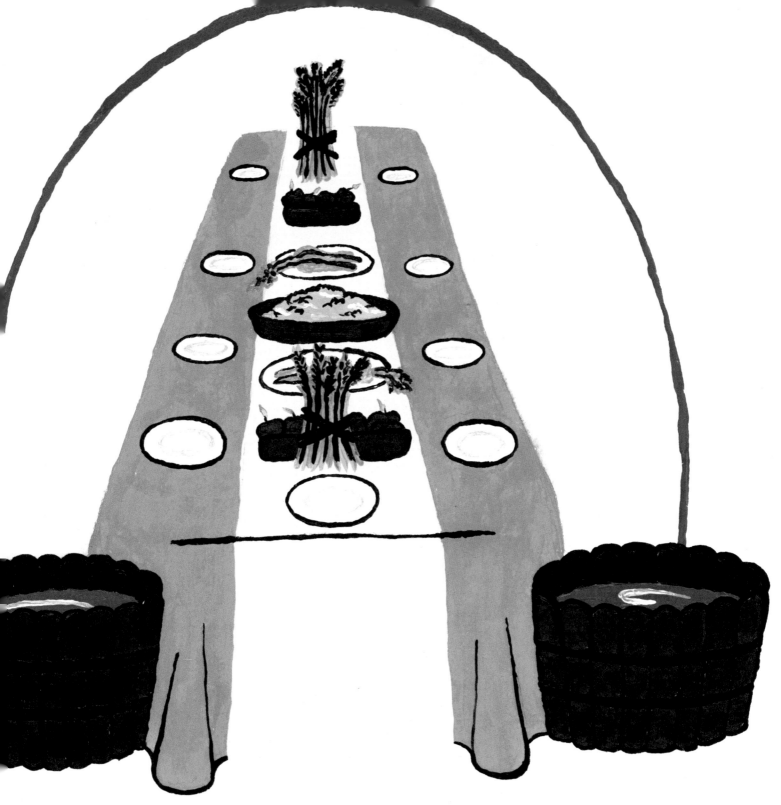

GYPSY

Gypsy gallops across the galaxy, hopping from star to star.

The galaxy whirls and twirls, connecting the dots.
A vision of a magical girl taking her shot.

Explore the cosmos–
A blank canvas for you to create a new space.

What a whirl! What a wonder!

The future is bright. Hang on tight!

FRIENDSHIP

You are my friend till the very end.
Thank you for loving me through health and mend.

Your hugs make everything better.

I look forward to a walk and a talk,
sharing time together through cries and goodbyes.

In busy times, no chance for a chat.
But you will be here when I get back.

We have the best of times.
You and me.

FROZEN

Asleep on his bed of powdered snow,
Frozen the unicorn awakes to the winter morning slow.

A world of white outside his palace.
A hush upon the land.

He throws on his silvery velvet cape
and decorates his long mane with icy roses and teal bows.

It's time to open the gates.

Disco lights fill the walls of all the halls,
the symphony sounds all around
while the glass lake awaits dancers and skaters.

Princess Ruby finally arrives.
Let the festivities begin!

At last, NUMBER TEN arrives.
Now the completed herd can play as they grow and thrive.

ENLIGHTEN

Awaken my child and listen.

Explore so you may know more.
Be brave. Be strong. Not a thing can go wrong.
All is as it was meant to be.

There is no doubt when you look inside yourself for answers.

Rise and shine, friend of mine.
Trust is a must.

Love is all the guidance you need.
Fog lifts to allow beams of light entry.
Sit for a while. Let's have tea.

SUNFLOWER UNICORN

SHOW NAME:
Circle G Georgie Porgie
BARN NAME:
George

RAINBOW UNICORN

SHOW NAME:
WCF Let Freedom Ring
BARN NAME:
Dove

GOOD KNIGHT UNICORN

SHOW NAME:
La Vista Allure by MG
BARN NAME:
Mardi

FREEDOM UNICORN

SHOW NAME:
Hallmarks Phantoms Vision
BARN NAME:
Phantom

BUTTERFLY UNICORN

SHOW NAME:
D&S Cashbacks Ramblin Rose
BARN NAME:
Rosey

WEDDING UNICORN

SHOW NAME:
Picture Perfect Honolulu Honey-
BARN NAME:
Aolani

GYPSY UNICORN

SHOW NAME:
JSW Redis Color of FameBARN
NAME:
Nemo

FROZEN UNICORN

SHOW NAME:
Alpha and Omega Stormy's Hero
BARN NAME:
Hogan

ENLIGHTEN UNICORN

SHOW NAME:
Mercedes Trick That
BARN NAME:
Ranger

FRIENDSHIP UNICORN

SHOW NAME:
Flyin Hearts Cocoa Bliss
BARN NAME:
Cocoa

Paige Clough is a passionate mother, teacher and lover of horses living in Katy, TX on her ranch, Paloma Trails, where she hosts riding and horse therapy programs for visitors of all ages and abilities.

Paige has loved horses since she was a young girl and, after her daughter showed an instinctive interest as a toddler, decided to devote her life to raising horses for all to enjoy.

The Ten Little Unicorns in her recently published children's book, "Ten Little Unicorns" are all part of a real herd of miniature horses living at Paloma Trails and brightening the lives of their visitors daily.

WWW.PALOMATRAILS.COM

Made in the USA
Columbia, SC
12 November 2022

71019041R00020